Death Strikes Back

Carolyn Marigold Stubbs

2QT Limited (Publishing)

First Edition published 2020 by
2QT Limited (Publishing)
Settle, North Yorkshire BD24 9BZ United Kingdom

This is a work of fiction and any resemblance to any person living or dead is purely coincidental. The place names mentioned may exist but have no connection with the events in this book

Cover Image © Carolyn Stubbs
Cover layout Hilary Pitt

Printed in Great Britain by Lightning Source UK LTD

Disclaimer
This is a work of fiction and any resemblance to any person living or dead is purely coincidental. The place names mentioned maybe real but have no connection with the events in this book

A CIP catalogue record for the paperback format book is available from the British Library
ISBN 978-1-913071-77-6

Preface

St Benedict's monastery in the southwest of England had been left in ruins following the Dissolution of the English monasteries in 1536 under King Henry VIII's reign. The wholesale destruction of priceless ecclesiastical treasures was regarded as possibly the greatest act of vandalism in English history. As monasteries were the wealthiest institutions in England and Wales, this act transformed the power structures of English society during those times.

Although historians debate the actual condition of the monasteries on the eve of the Dissolution and the various motivations behind the act, there is no doubt that it changed the face of the land. The luckiest of these once sacred houses were lavishly remodelled as private residences; others fell into disrepair and crumbled to nothing.

Many former monasteries were sold off to local landowners while others were taken over and subsequently became churches, Durham Cathedral being one example. Monks who resisted were often executed but those who surrendered were usually spared their lives. Many beautiful structures were left to decay, their riches brutally taken, such as the beautiful Cistercian abbey of Tintern, one of the greatest monastic ruins of Wales.

In this hostile and dangerous climate, the monks of St Benedict's in Dorset left their abbey and fled to the safety of the continent, where they formed a new community. The abbey's stonework survived remarkably well over the years, leaving intact a distinct tracery of the ribs of the ruins. Even decades later, it was still possible to visualise the abbey as it had been designed originally. The roof of the abbey, however, had been pillaged in order to recover the valuable lead.

Over the decades, more tolerant times eventually returned. A wealthy local landowner, who was also devoutly religious, was able to purchase the ruins of St Benedict's and its surrounding acres of land.

The landowner's ancestors managed to retain their wealth following the Dissolution by ostensibly buying (on paper at least) the land where the monastery was left in ruins. Finally, when the time was right and it was safe to do so, the monastery was rebuilt based on the original design. There were some valuable additions such as the stained glass windows, the ornamental portal to the chapter house and bespoke sculptures of the twelve apostles.

Monastic life resumed once again and followed the earlier traditions of strict Benedictine rules. The brotherhood began to grow in numbers and the land that had fallen to barren waste was lovingly restored. Cultivated and nurtured, it provided food and wine to sustain the diligent monks who tended it. They were able to sell their products commercially, which provided a much-needed income for repairs and the ongoing maintenance of the abbey.

As a fully-functioning working monastery, St Benedict's wasn't open to the general public so it was not included as a tourist venue. Yet, despite infrequent visits from the outside world, the brotherhood always adhered to the rules of St Benedict: no one was ever refused help and refuge, if warranted, and all were made welcome.

Chapter One

I was a stranger and you welcomed me. (Matthew 25:35)
All guests are to be welcomed as Christ. (Rule of St Benedict Chapter 53)

It had just gone midnight when the peace and tranquillity of St Benedict's Monastery were suddenly shattered by the sounds of someone frantically banging on the main outer door. The small community of brothers had long retired to bed for the night, but even the heaviest sleepers were awoken by the noisy racket echoing as it did through the winding, draughty passages of the ancient monastery.

Brother James pushed back his bed covers and sat up, rubbing his eyes. Blinking away sleep, he turned on his bedside light and looked at the clock: 12:02, the glowing red digital numbers informed him. The monastery was used to having callers now and again but, tucked away and hidden deep in the heart of the Dorset countryside, it was a very rare event and had never occurred before at this late hour.

So it was with some apprehension that he rose from the warmth and comfort of his bed to face whoever was causing such a commotion. Putting on his outer robe and slipping his feet into old worn sandals, he left his cell and strode anxiously towards the door.

Following close on his heels were Brothers Luke and Peter, two portly men in their late sixties, concern etched on their faces. 'Who on earth could it be at this time of night?' whispered Brother Peter hesitantly, aware that he was breaking the rigid vows of night silence. Breaking that vow was only permitted in exceptional circumstances – like these, he reassured himself.

The hammering hadn't abated; if anything, it had become even louder and more insistent. As they approached the entrance, they heard someone calling out in obvious distress. Peering through the spy-hole in the door, Brother James could see the figure of a highly agitated man who was breathing rapidly, although his features were hidden in the gloom of the night.

The heavy cast-iron door knocker was rammed against the wood of the door again and again as the man's voice pleaded, 'Please let me in! Please! I have nowhere to go! Help me, I'm begging you. I just can't take any more! My life is ruined.' Then the voice started to peter out and the brothers heard muffled sobs.

Woken by the commotion, more of the brotherhood had now assembled. Still half asleep, they clustered together in the chilly inner vestibule looking anxiously towards the door yet remaining silent.

Brother James slowly drew back the sturdy bolts and, turning a weighty brass key, felt the door unlock with an audible click. Grasping the handle, he cautiously pulled it open.

The lights from within the vestibule shone out onto weathered flagstones to reveal the dishevelled figure of a man, shivering and clutching a small holdall. Unshaven and with matted hair, he wore a thin, grimy coat that was obviously the worse for wear. He looked completely exhausted.

Brother James stretched out his arms in welcome. 'Come on in, please, and let us see how we may be of help.'

'I'm so sorry to wake you, but I didn't know what else to do,' the stranger blurted out. All eyes were upon the man as he stepped wearily inside.

Closing the door behind him, Brother James smiled reassuringly. 'Come this way, my friend, and do not be afraid. Whatever your plight, we will do our best to help you.'

'Thank you,' said the stranger with a wan smile. Suddenly he went very pale and reeled, as if he were about to pass out. Brother James and Brother Peter quickly supported him on either side, whilst relieving him of his holdall.

'We'll go to the chapter house,' said Brother James. Turning to the assembled monks, who were still standing in the hallway, he said, 'Thank you, Brothers, but we can manage now. We don't want to overwhelm our guest so I suggest you all go back to bed and get some rest.'

They nodded and obeyed dutifully, returning silently to their cells.

Chapter Two

The monastery rule for admitting those who called there was unequivocal and it flashed through the brothers' minds: 'I came as a guest, and you received Me. Let all guests who arrive be received like Christ, and let all due honour be.'

'Do you think we should we wake up Abbott Alwin?' asked Brother Peter, clearly anxious at this unprecedented event.

'No, not at this stage,' replied Brother James. 'There's no point in disturbing him at this hour. We'll leave it until the morning, when hopefully we'll have a better picture of this troubled man's situation.'

The stranger's head was bowed and he made no eye contact with them; it was almost as if he were feeling ashamed.

The chapter house lay within the monastery. It was a place where the monks met every day to discuss business and be reminded of their strict monastic rules as they listened to readings from *Regula Benedicti*. It was the most appropriate and obvious choice to take any guest, invited or uninvited.

They walked slowly towards the east wing of the cloister until they arrived at the magnificent entrance to the chapter house. The portal was a door with an elaborate façade. Trails of highly decorated archivolts adorned the arched doorway in a ribbon of tiny, exquisite sculptures. On either side of the portal were carved figures of the twelve apostles. It was an aesthetic vision of immense beauty. The vaulted ceiling, with its lofty Romanesque arches, added to its splendour, and spectacular stained-glass windows, painted frescoes and many striking artworks graced the room.

As they entered the chapter house, the stranger, who had not spoken a word since being welcomed into the monastery, gasped as he took in its magnificence. 'I am truly in the house of God,' he exclaimed.

Moonlight flooded in through one of the stained-glass windows, casting muted patterns and irregular soft shadows on the thick stone walls. A large fireplace still contained remnants of glowing red embers. Brother Peter quickly added more wood from the pile of logs stacked against the hearth and the fire crackled into life again. As was the Benedictine custom before officially receiving any visitor, prayers were said. Brother James led them towards the altar and knelt before it.

The ethos of Benedictine monasteries was always to ensure that sufficient food was readily available for anyone who came to them in need of sustenance or shelter. Growing their own food, making their wine and spending long hours each day in prayer, the monks rarely ventured into the outside world, yet they always had abundant food and grain stocks.

After prayers, Brother Peter went to the kitchen and returned with a tray laden with bread, cheeses and a jug of red wine. The brothers and the stranger sat down on one of the fine wooden benches that was painstakingly carved with trails of curling leaves; it was highly polished, leaving a lingering aroma of honeyed beeswax.

Resting plates on their laps, they ate quietly. The stranger tucked in ravenously. Supping the strong red wine, they all began to feel more relaxed. The fire emitted a comforting warmth, the atmosphere had mellowed, and the stranger seemed more at ease as the food and wine ran through his veins.

'Tell me,' asked Brother James gently, 'what misfortune has led you to us, that you should arrive so distressed and needing our assistance so late at night?'

The stranger sat silently for a minute or two, as if composing himself before embarking upon his story. He ran his fingers through his hair then he started to speak hesitantly in a thin voice. 'My name is Georgio Stephano. First of all, I must thank you from the bottom of my heart for allowing me to enter your monastery. I am Italian and was born in the beautiful city of Florence. Before coming to this country, I spent considerable time in the priesthood. That is why I approached you.' He looked up at them and his dark, brooding eyes seemed to hope they would understand.

'Take your time, Georgio. We are not interrogating you,' said Brother James kindly. 'We are just trying to make ourselves familiar with your situation. Are you still a priest?'

'Not any more. It is rather a long story, so I will try and make it as short as I can for you. Five years ago, I left my native land of Italy, my family and my life as a priest to work in a well-respected British institution. The work involved the archiving and restoration of ancient manuscripts, something I was passionate about and had experience of whilst I was in the priesthood.'

Georgio took another sip of wine and gazed into the fire, his eyes full of sorrow. 'I must have disappointed my family. They are devout Roman Catholics and I had joined the priesthood and followed in the footsteps of my two older brothers, as was expected. The idea had been indoctrinated in me from such an early age that my career path was already planned out by the time I reached adulthood.'

'Was the priesthood something you wanted to do, Georgio?' asked Brother Peter.

'I believed it was. I just accepted it because the idea had been planted in me as long as I could remember. It wasn't until I discovered that I had a natural aptitude for learning that I started to question it.'

Georgio told them that preparing for the priesthood in Italy was a big commitment, requiring eight years of study beyond high school and a college degree. 'It didn't stop there,' he added. 'I had several more demanding academic periods in my life, including theology, of course, which I studied at a seminary.'

From what Georgio was telling them it appeared that, although he came across as a modest man, he was a gifted academic who had excelled in the classics, Latin and ancient history.

Chapter Three

Georgio Stephano's work had received the highest praise. His book, *The History and Preservation of the Illuminated Manuscript*, was his first written piece and became one of the hallmarks of his success. It wasn't long before he was in huge demand for lectures on that subject. After leaving the priesthood, and because of his unique and specialised experience, Georgio quickly managed to attain a position within a respected British institution that involved archiving and restoring ancient manuscripts.

'When I left Italy five years ago,' he told the brothers, 'I didn't feel sad because I truly believed I was on the road to a better life. Things were working out very well for me. I was going to do a job I loved and for which I was qualified. I wanted to embrace the British way of life and immerse myself in its culture, so later I became a British citizen.'

It was while he was delivering one of his lectures that he met Gabrielle, a senior college librarian who caught his eye immediately. Tall and willowy, with flaming red hair, she exuded beauty, intelligence and wit; it was an instant and mutual attraction. There followed a brief, highly-charged, romantic and passionate liaison. They read the same books, shared the same taste in music and it wasn't long before they fell deeply in love. Georgio had little experience with women before Gabrielle; he'd had a couple of girlfriends after he had arrived in the UK but nothing serious. This new chapter in his romantic life was all-consuming.

Three months later, after a whirlwind romance, they were married. 'Gabrielle was the absolute love of my life and she made me so happy,' he told them. 'My career was taking off and I was with the most wonderful woman. I'd never felt so fulfilled. Everything was perfect – a dream wife, a dream job…'

Georgio faltered; his face clouded over and his eyes welled up with tears.

There was a sudden gust of wind and the windows rattled above them. The candles flickered and the temperature seemed to drop. 'Let's put some more logs on the fire,' said Brother Peter. 'It has chilled down considerably, and we must make sure you are comfortable and warm.' After he piled on more logs, the fire crackled into a blaze of heat, giving the three of them a comforting warm glow which was much needed in the draughty chapter house.

'Do continue,' said Brother James encouragingly, noting the anguish on Georgio's pale face.

'I became very absorbed in my work,' the stranger continued. 'Also, following the publication of my book, there was an increasing demand for talks and lectures. Somehow I failed to notice subtle warning signs about our marriage that, in hindsight, I shouldn't have ignored. Gabrielle had always accompanied me to the talks I gave. Sitting in the front row, her lovely face smiling approvingly, she would clap with unrestrained enthusiasm and be so supportive. Yet some months later, there always seemed to be a reason why she couldn't come with me. She blamed increased work pressures, reorganisation of the staffing structure, meetings. They seemed valid reasons so I just accepted them without question.'

Georgio ruefully admitted that they had spent little quality time together in those last few months. Working long hours, giving lectures and talks in the evening, there was never enough time in the day. When he arrived home late, he'd jump into bed, fall asleep, then get up early the next day only to start the whole process all over again. He had become absorbed in his work to the detriment of his relationship with the beautiful woman at his side; he had become complacent and taken her love and company for granted.

'We barely see each other these days,' she had told him. 'A snatch of conversation here and a peck on the cheek there. What sort of life is this?'

The early morning light was now filtering through the windows as night began to slip away. The last remnants of the fire gave little warmth now but the Brothers still sat patiently in the cooling air, listening as Georgio continued his story.

'Those words alone should have been enough of a warning but stupidly I ignored them, telling her this was only a temporary phase and in the years to come we'd have plenty of time together. But somehow she couldn't seem to accept that. She felt lonely, unhappy at how things were. It wasn't what she'd expected of married life.'

As weeks went by following that conversation, Gabrielle became more distant. She was always busy with things that Georgio wasn't involved in. Then one day when he arrived back from work she was in the living room, waiting for him with a grim expression on her face.

Georgio began to sob as he re-lived the moment, tears streaming down his face. 'She told me she was leaving me. Nothing I could do or say would change her mind. Her bags were already packed, her suitcases resting against the sofa. I begged her, pleaded with her, got down on my knees and told her I would even throw away my career if it meant she'd give me another chance.' The hurt on Georgio's face was etched starkly, as if it had been carved in stone.

Gabrielle was resolute in her decision.

'If I'd been less interested in my success and had taken more notice of what was going on in my marriage, then this might never have happened. It could possibly and should have been avoided,' Georgio said morosely.

Chapter Four

Yet things were to become even worse, he told them. After she'd gone, his career, his faith, everything he had once considered precious, seemed totally unimportant. He couldn't focus on anything; his mind was elsewhere. The vows they had made in church, the plans they'd had for the future, seemed like a dream as if they had never happened.

'I began drinking heavily to try and numb the pain,' he told the brothers. 'I would sit watching television all day, wasting time, consuming copious amounts of alcohol and getting more and more depressed. I just didn't care what happened to me any more.' Georgio started to sob again, his body taut with emotion.

Brother James patted his shoulder. 'Although I have never loved a woman, I can remember the love that I had for my family so, in some small way, I have a grain of understanding of what terrible pain you must have experienced. Heartbreak is the most painful of emotions, I believe.'

Georgio nodded. 'Day after dreary day I woke up feeling terrible. A darkness enveloped my soul. After constantly turning up late at the institute and failing to complete the restoration of my manuscript on time, I was given several stark warnings. I know that my employers were trying their best to help me, and they showed enormous patience, but I couldn't focus on my work. I didn't even have the will to try.'

This ultimately cost him his valued position at the acclaimed Institute of Restored Manuscripts. His self-esteem plummeted even further and his reputation was in shreds.

'Was there no family member you could turn to?' Brother James asked.

'Oh no,' Georgio replied, horrified. 'I was so ashamed of my failures that I hid them. To all intents and purposes, my family back in Italy thought I was working and happily married to Gabrielle. They hinted at the prospect of a grandchild sometime in the future! How could I tell them? The son they were so proud of had got himself into such a dreadful mess – and it was all of my own making.'

'What about friends? Was there anyone close to you who could have helped you?'

'Not really. I suppose that I didn't have any particularly close friends because I'd been in the priesthood. And, after my position was terminated, I felt too ashamed to approach my former work colleagues. Gabrielle was the one with lots of friends but obviously, after she left me, they were gone too.'

'So what has brought you to us now, Georgio?' asked Brother Peter.

'I've lost everything precious to me, including my self-respect. That's why I became addicted to gambling, something I'd never believed could happen to me,' he mumbled.

Whilst filling empty hours scrolling aimlessly on his computer, he had come across a gambling website. It started harmlessly enough but the thrill of a win was compelling. He was distracted by a brand-new emotion, different from the crushing emptiness that had engulfed him. He couldn't get enough.

Seeing an advertisement for a new casino that had recently opened, proved to be too much of a temptation for Georgio to resist. With a wad of overdrawn bank notes in his pocket, gambling quickly became the new love of his life. The buzz and excitement were such distractions from his personal circumstances that soon he could not stop. He was in another world. Even when he was losing vast sums of money on a daily basis, money that he couldn't repay, gambling was such an escape that he would stay in the casino until the small hours. The pain was gone, replaced by excitement and the desperation to win. It made him feel completely out of touch with reality; in this new environment, he could blot out everything and forget.

'Although I had some small wins at the start, I regularly lost. The amounts increased day by day, hour by hour. I was paying with credit I didn't have, and the reality of what was happening just seemed to elude me. I was in another world, so very different from my former life. Even though I knew what I was doing was wrong, I couldn't stop. But, as my lessons in the priesthood had taught me so clearly, I remembered the warning in Numbers 32:23, "be sure your sins will find you out". I deserved what was in store for me. I had broken every vow I'd ever made and my inflated ego had lost me Gabrielle.'

Eventually the bank, along with many other organisations that Georgio owed money to, sent him increasingly stronger reminders. He faced mounting bills, gambling debts that he could not repay. His bank account, drastically overdrawn, was frozen. There were more notices, more final warnings, but still Georgio ignored them.

Finally, it came to the point where his house was repossessed. His entire world, and the person that he had once been, were gone. There was nothing left. 'I felt like a sinking ship with no lifeboat in sight. All the light from my life had turned into darkness and despair. I felt this overriding urge to run and run and run. I had to escape.'

Chapter Five

Georgio Stephano was a different man from the one who had arrived at the Benedictine monastery some five years earlier. Then he had been a complete mental and physical wreck. The abbot had immediately accepted him, no questions asked, and it was there that he finally found a sanctuary for his grief-stricken soul.

Despite everything that had happened, and although he had begun questioning why so much tragedy had befallen him, Stephano was still a man of deep faith. He knew he couldn't have survived those early months but for the protected environment of the brotherhood. Nevertheless, he felt enormous guilt that he'd used the monastery as an escape from his failures in life. He also knew that sooner or later, he would have to find a way to repay the enormous sums of money he owed.

For the first couple of years, he had allowed himself to heal as much as possible. He involved himself in the work of the monastery and he positively welcomed the menial daily routine because of the security it gave him. Tending the vegetable garden, helping with housekeeping duties and assisting in the production of the monastery's wine distracted him and allowed some respite from his problems. But he knew he would never get over the loss of his wife, the pain of betrayal by his one and only true love who had so brutally abandoned him. He knew that ultimately this would shorten his life and send him to an early grave. No one can suffer so much pain without it having a profound effect upon the body, mind and soul, he told himself.

Georgio Stephano's conscience ultimately decided for him: he couldn't remain any longer in this cushion of comfort where he had been welcomed, given support and unquestioning kindness for five long years. After deliberating for some months, he summoned up the courage to make an appointment to see the abbot. He had to explain and justify his reasons for leaving this protected way of life, despite his reluctance to go.

He hadn't entered the brotherhood for altruistic reasons and, because of his faith, he needed to address and face the consequences of his former actions.

He walked along the west cloister, with its ancient cobbled flooring and Gothic pointed arches. It led directly to the main part of the monastery where Abbot Alwin resided. Reaching the top of the stairs, Georgio paused for a moment. He felt nervous. His heart raced as he pressed the buzzer, a polished brass button mounted on a large oak door. After a couple of minutes, which seemed like an eternity, he heard the deep timbre of the revered abbot's voice. 'Enter.'

Abbot Alwin was sitting on a leather armchair beside a large window that overlooked the lush grounds of the monastery. There were fine views of softly undulating hills in the far distance. He was wearing a plain black clerical robe with a large golden crucifix hanging loosely around his neck.

He beckoned Georgio towards him warmly. 'Come, sit down next to me, Brother, and tell me what's on your mind.' With a flourish he pointed to the empty chair opposite him and looked kindly at the nervous young man.

'Thank you, Father,' Georgio replied weakly, easing himself into the plush cushioned armchair. Abbot Alwin smiled, waiting patiently for him to speak. After giving a slight cough and nervously shifting in his seat, Georgio finally said, 'I'm sorry, Father, but I can't carry on the pretence any longer. You know, through my various confessions, why I became a monk. It wasn't for the right reasons, despite me once being a Catholic priest. I did not join you for selfless or spiritual reasons. I must thank you and all of the brotherhood so very much for your understanding, your patience and your generosity of spirit for allowing me to stay under circumstances that were purely for my own benefit.'

The abbot gazed sympathetically at Georgio, then reached out and patted his hand. 'Don't be so hard on yourself. I know and fully understand the troubles you have had in your life. Do not think for one minute that you've been selfish. You are a deeply spiritual person whom everyone has warmed to. I also know that there is a kind and contrite person behind that often impermeable wall you put up. You have contributed so much to the brotherhood during your time here that we will be sad to see you go.'

Georgio's eyes opened wide in amazement. He hadn't expected a

written many books about world faiths, historical saints and martyrs. He was an acclaimed and respected expert in his field.

There was also no doubt about the immense value of the ring that weighed heavily on Georgio's finger. He remembered the strange burst of energy that came to him when he first took it out of the box. Had he imagined that? He wasn't sure now.

Acutely aware of the glittering gemstones on his finger and the journey he was about to take using public transport, he discreetly put his hands in his pockets and turned his thoughts to his immediate future. The monastery had helped him get a decent teaching post at a private school. It paid reasonably well, and the modest bedsit he'd acquired was conveniently located close by. It was a new start, a chance to begin repaying some of the enormous debts he owed and an opportunity to shed some of the guilt he carried.

He was unsure how often he should wear the precious ring but decided that he would place his faith in what the abbot told him. As the chosen wearer, he would wear it at all times, but he would keep it hidden when teaching or going to places where it would look ostentatious.

Georgio had been given another opportunity because of the generosity of the brotherhood. He felt a glint of optimism but he was wary of building up any hopes of joy; he was still tortured by overwhelming sadness for the loss of his beloved wife. Happiness was a faint and distant memory – but whatever was in store for him couldn't be any worse than that which he had already been through.

Chapter Seven

The Regent Palace Casino owners hadn't forgotten about the large sums of money that Georgio Stephano still owed them. They frequently granted credit to gamblers who provided evidence of sizeable bank accounts to cover their IOUs, or if they had a credit history with the casino that indicated they had repaid their debts. Initially, Georgio's credit rating had been good and he had had sufficient funds in the bank to repay his debts. Since that time, however, all casinos had tightened their policies. These were no longer boom years when casinos could absorb losses easily and gamblers had plenty of money to spend.

Georgio Stephano had received an interest-free loan from the casino with flexible terms. It was an unusual feature in the business world and a unique risk for casinos, which wrote off as much as five per cent of their debts, sometimes amounting to millions of pounds a year, as uncollectable. However, the Regent Palace Casino had always fought hard to reclaim its losses whenever they could. If the debtor couldn't repay in money, sometimes they had to pay in other ways. The casino's tough stance was a warning to others – pay up or else!

It had been hard to track down Georgio Stephano as he had literally vanished for five years and no trace of him could be found. Finally, however, the casino's monitoring service picked up new activity in Stephano's bank account triggered by a couple of cheque payments sent to their accounts department.

'At a measly £25 a month, it would take more than a lifetime to clear the debt,' the accountants complained in disgust. If Georgio Stephano thought that this paltry amount would placate the casino, then he was mistaken!

Georgio's life soon fell into a comfortable routine. He regularly taught Latin and Classics to a talented bunch of sixth formers. His salary allowed him to pay a fixed, albeit small, amount back to the casino and to his other creditors. Otherwise he ate frugally, spent very little on himself and wore the mysterious ring when circumstances allowed.

He was extremely grateful for all the help and support he had received from the abbot and brothers at the monastery. They had helped him to find a modest but clean and tidy basement flat in a quiet area of town. The location was ideal for work as a bus took him almost door to door. For his spiritual nourishment and confessions, he never failed to attend the services at his local church, St Anselm's.

One night he again joined the ever-diminishing congregation for the weekly Tuesday prayer meeting. Georgio found St Anselm's an inspiring place. A calm came over him inside the ancient church, which was filled with icons, religious paintings and glorious stained-glass windows. He prayed for forgiveness, as he always did, and promised to atone for his past mistakes. He also prayed earnestly that the immense, overbearing pain of loss and betrayal would eventually leave him. He felt that he could not carry this burden for very much longer. There was no colour in his life since Gabrielle had gone, just a dismal bleak grey monotone, a blanket of misery.

After the parish priest, Father O'Leary, had collected his belongings, he walked back down the main aisle of the church. He gave a last backward glance at the kneeling figure of Georgio Stephano. As usual, Georgio was deeply engrossed in prayer, hands clenched and body taut. Father O'Leary had tried everything he could think of to help the poor man and was at a loss how to ease his pain. Perhaps in time Georgio would be able to move on, to find some kind of peace; as he was more deserving of it than many.

Sighing in resignation, the priest stepped out into the chilly night air and closed the heavy wooden doors behind him.

Chapter Eight

Concealed in the shadowy recesses of the east transept of the church was Patrick Stone, a hired professional assassin. Dressed completely in black, with a hooded top pulled up over his head, his features were barely visible in the mellow candlelight. He had been crouching behind one of the huge granite pillars, hiding there for some considerable time before the service had begun.

This latest assignment – the ending of a life in a church – was a first for Stone, and it made him even more enthusiastic than usual. The prospect of the ritualistic killing of a former priest appealed to him enormously. Stone enjoyed his work; he'd done it many times and he luxuriated in the great sense of accomplishment it gave him. Yet he took a cold, calculating, almost clinical approach to his work and carried out the executions with meticulous attention to detail.

Stone knew that he was extremely good at what he did. He always added his own signature to his assignments and he liked to embellish his executions with more than a hint of drama. He took great satisfaction in designing an appropriate style of elimination for each of his victims. The method he used had to fit in with the particular person he was contracted to kill, their identity and role in life; it was an essential ingredient for Stone, for he was the architect of their demise.

The assassination would match the person's lifestyle, their unique environment or their workplace. Delivering the final death throes by using his chosen method gave him an inordinate sense of power. Attention to detail was his hallmark; the mastery of his craft had earned him great respect in the criminal underworld and there was no one to match him.

Stone recalled his most recent job. He had assassinated a financial director while he worked late into the night at his office. The businessman could never have imagined how his death would become front-page news. As with each case, planning was everything and Stone had done his groundwork well in advance. He knew his victim's movements and daily routines intimately, as well as the office security systems and level of staff. By hacking into the office server and accessing files, he was able to discover the times when the director would be alone.

He remembered wondering if the financial director would turn around just before he was attacked. But no; he was focused on the spreadsheets on his computer, the victim was killed instantly by a deadly blow to the back of the head . With Stone's flair for the dramatic, he'd added final touches to the scene. He felt these 'touches' matched the person, his world and his environment. Securing the body to a swivel chair, Stone had filled the victim's mouth with a mixture of rolled banknotes and heavy coins. He had prepared and enlarged a blank cheque with the words 'Payment Received Thank You', which he pinned onto the lapel of the director's Savile Row suit jacket. His intricate planning ensured that the director would not be found until the following morning by his personal secretary. Stone felt that the scene would be exquisite: in the midst of that mighty powerhouse of money and fortune would be her dead boss, powerful no more!

These theatrical embellishments fed Stone's already enormous ego, and his feelings of superiority grew with each assignment. So far, the police authorities hadn't even come close to catching up with him.

Now Stone was fingering his chosen weapon with a feeling of smug satisfaction. He'd selected this particular method of execution with care. As with previous assignments, planning was everything. This was one of the reasons he believed he had never been caught, or even become a suspect. He had ended so many lives but, even with the latest forensic methods of finding and collecting evidence, he had escaped detection.

Although Stone was looking forward to the novelty of ending a life in the hallowed confines of a church, it made him unnaturally anxious. This was a completely different assignment because the victim was not actually a criminal but someone who'd got himself heavily into debt – and for the first time, by all accounts.

Religion and any forms of morality were alien concepts to Stone, yet there was something about this job that didn't quite stack up. Death was a heavy price to pay for a few thousand pounds, he thought. Nonetheless, he'd accepted the assignment and he was going to do it with the usual

Patrick Stone style.

Reaching into the right-hand pocket of his coat, Stone slid his hand over the weapon he'd carefully selected for this former priest – an eighteenth-century, silver-hilted Persian dagger. It was beautifully crafted, slender, with a razor-sharp curved blade: a thing of beauty, a work of art. The hilt was decorated with fine swirling filigree and it resonated with the antiquity of the church and its ancient relics. His victim was privileged that Stone had gone out of his way to obtain the weapon; no one else would have gone to so much trouble.

'Think yourself very lucky, Georgio,' Stone whispered under his breath with a grim smile. He'd also planned that this assassination would take place in the church, a fitting location for the former priest to meet his end, he thought.

Bought from a trusted Internet source that dealt in fine antique weapons, the Persian dagger had been despatched to one of Stone's numerous post-office boxes. When ordering online, Stone always used a public computer in an Internet café and he never used the same one twice. He ensured there was no electronic paper trail, never published any details of himself on websites, and the persona he had created was completely false. His careful precautions protected his true identity. Extremely clever, and with a devious mind, his analytical approach ensured that failure was a word that never, ever entered his vocabulary.

Chapter Nine

Furtively, Stone watched his victim's kneeling figure, which had barely moved since the prayer meeting finished. He had kept him under surveillance for the past few weeks, trailing him, keeping a record of his movements and noting his punctuality. Georgio was a good timekeeper and it seemed he never arrived late for anything. Three times a week he could be found here, attending the prayer sessions. He was also a man who liked his routines, remaining behind after each service long after everyone else had left.

Generally, there was only a small handful of people in the congregation and today had been no different, except perhaps there were even fewer people than the previous week. What a complete and utter waste of time, Stone thought; hardly worth opening up the church for. So much for religion – it certainly wasn't going to do Georgio any good, he chuckled to himself. Where was God when you needed him?

Although the church was now empty, Stone still double-checked for any last signs of movement or sounds. He looked back into the darkened areas and was satisfied that, following Father O'Leary's departure, the church was completely deserted apart from himself and his intended victim.

Flowers from a recent burial service filled the air with heavy scents, and the golden glow of the candles added to the stillness and quiet peace of this consecrated place. The mood was soon to be altered, thought Stone, a thought that amused him.

Swiftly and silently, like a black panther stalking his prey, Stone crept up behind Georgio Stephano's kneeling, bent frame. As his gloved hands unsheathed the dagger, he could hear the former priest chanting quietly under his breath, totally immersed in his prayers and meditation. Without hesitation, Stone grabbed Georgio's head and, holding it in a tight lock, quickly drew the cruel blade across his victim's throat.

Georgio cried out briefly as the weapon sliced effortlessly into his flesh, creating a wide gaping wound. Blood spurted out in an instant, a deep crimson fountain that flowed copiously from his neck. The once-kneeling figure now slumped forward heavily, crumpling slowly into a heap on the cold, mosaic-tiled floor, his precious life rapidly ebbing away.

Stone carefully wiped the blade on Georgio's blood-stained jacket. That was almost too easy, he thought, no fighting back, no struggling. He'd taken his victim completely by surprise. He carefully laid the dagger beside Georgio's dead body. With a book of psalms he had gathered up earlier, Stone placed it under one of the lifeless, outstretched hands.

Stone stood back for a moment, taking stock of the dramatic scene of carnage that he had created. He felt pleased with how well his mission had gone, and he took out his camera to capture the evidence. He always took several digital images immediately after finishing an assignment. This was his first-hand proof of a job completed before it reached any of the newspapers or local media. It also ensured prompt payment.

Checking the pictures through the camera's viewfinder, he saw that he had taken enough clear images. However, something unusual caught Stone's attention on the very last picture. On Georgio's outstretched hand, a large ring of great brilliance glinted brightly on his finger, catching the light of the flickering candles. Stone immediately went over to check it.

Carefully stepping over the sticky pool of blood that was rapidly collecting, Stone cautiously examined the ring on Georgio's still-warm finger. With his gloved hands, he carefully slid it off. He was astonished at its mesmerising beauty; he had never come across anything like this before. It had an almost ethereal quality, yet even the most inexperienced eye could tell at once that it was of immense value. It was a complete mystery that this pious man should be in possession of such a ring, a man who was bankrupt only five years ago, who owed so much money and who lived so frugally.

Where on earth had Georgio Stephano acquired such a fabulous treasure, and why hadn't he sold it to pay off his debts? It would have been the solution to so many of his problems. But these were questions that Stone didn't have the answers to. For now, he pocketed the item, aware that time was moving on and he had to make his escape.

He was mindful that the churchwarden would be arriving soon, so there was no time to lose. Taking a last careful look around the scene, he checked for any detail he might have overlooked, any tiny shred of incriminating evidence that might link him to the crime. But no, everything was clear. Satisfied with his final checks, he walked briskly out of the church. This assignment would go down as one of his most memorable, he thought.

He needed to return home quickly, take a shower and dispose of the clothes he was wearing before catching the night train to Liverpool.

Stepping out into the cool night air, Stone was relieved to find the side street beside the church devoid of people. Even so, he walked briskly, taking the well-rehearsed shortcut to his temporary accommodation. A couple of hours later, he emerged from a small terraced house transformed from his previous black-hooded attire into that of a respectable businessman. Even dressed smartly, in a dark pinstriped suit and expensive navy trench coat, with his hair oiled and slicked back, Stone's eyes displayed a steely hardness that was rarely seen in a man. With his laptop and briefcase in hand, he headed for the busy main road and hailed a passing taxi.

Arriving at the railway station, Stone glanced anxiously at his watch. The train would be leaving in less than five minutes and he couldn't afford to miss it. He hadn't anticipated the unexpected road works that had slowed down his journey. His pre-bought tickets were in his wallet, but still he wondered whether he would make it. This was the very last train that night to his destination.

Thrusting a generous wad of notes at the cab driver, he sprinted out of the taxi bay and raced across the concourse. Relieved, he saw his train was still standing at the platform. The illuminated clock showed just two minutes left before departure!

Stone's breath was laboured and his heart was racing. Reaching the nearest door, he hauled himself up the step and clambered into the carriage.

Chapter Ten

A guard immediately slammed the door shut behind him, the whistle blew and, with a sudden lurch, the train began to move and gradually gain speed. Stone leaned back momentarily against the carriage door to catch his breath. As his pulse rate returned to normal, he made his way through the connecting carriages towards the first-class section. His seat reservation showed that he was in coach H; when he reached it, he found that there were only four other occupants. That came as a relief. The last thing he wanted was to make polite conversation with anyone or attract undue attention to himself.

A woman in her thirties with boyish short-cropped hair was tapping away at a laptop a couple of rows away. Further down the carriage, a studious-looking couple in their late twenties were both reading. They cast a cursory glance in Stone's direction before returning their attention to their books. The fourth passenger was older, a man somewhere in his late forties with grey receding hair. His charcoal-grey suit jacket lay neatly across the seat next to him. Busy writing up notes and drinking a beer, he glanced up briefly and seemed to barely notice Stone's arrival.

Stone eased himself wearily into his reserved seat. For the first time in his line of work, he felt that he'd made a glaring error. He had only managed to catch this train by the skin of his teeth; he'd been complacent and should have checked on the traffic reports beforehand. He had been fortunate this time, but never again would he allow slip-ups like that to occur, he told himself. Yet the actual execution had gone exactly to plan, and he took immense pleasure from the scene he had left behind. The ancient dagger that took the life of the former priest and the book of psalms that lay next to the body would soon be discovered in the quiet stillness of the church.

The dramatic setting that he had implemented with such precision would rank as one of his finest. He couldn't wait to hear about it on the news; the media would have a field day with this one, he smirked. He was certain that the authorities would never be able to trace him. Frustratingly for the police, his hallmark signature in this crime would link it to many other unsolved murders, blatantly reminding them of his continued ability to elude them.

Peering out into the blackness of the night, Stone saw the bright lights of offices and shops flashing past in the distance. He spread his belongings onto the vacant seat beside him and, settling himself into a comfortable position, started to think about his meeting the next day. When the assignment was approved and signed over to his client, he would collect a handsome sum of money and return home a much wealthier man. His reputation in the criminal underworld would be enhanced once again, and he could look forward to raising his fees substantially for his next mission. He would be in an even better position to choose the work he would accept and he could afford to turn down the jobs that held little or no interest. By raising his fees, he knew that respect for his work would be rewarded and acknowledged. It was always a matter of pride for Patrick Stone.

He could retire easily on the money he had accumulated over the years, together with the significant amount he was due to collect in the morning. Also, he now had that precious ring in his possession and he knew just where to get the best price for it. But retiring was out of the question; he wouldn't, and couldn't, give up something that gave him so much pleasure. His life was exciting and challenging. Each project was different and had its own set of problems to overcome – and that in itself was part of the enjoyment for Stone. There was the painstaking planning and preparation for each new job, then there was the huge adrenalin rush of the kill and finally the pleasure of outwitting the police. No, he would never retire, never give it up; the money was secondary for him.

A wave of tiredness hit Stone and, coupled with the motion of the train, it soon led him to drift off to sleep. Twenty minutes later he was woken up by the noisy hiss of the inter-connecting door that led into the carriage. A couple of teenage girls had burst in by mistake. Giggling, they rushed back out again and the door closed automatically behind them.

Stone, now wide awake, decided to take another look at his pictures of Georgio Stephano's corpse. As far as he could tell, there was no CCTV in this carriage; however, he still took the precaution of angling himself into the corner and positioning himself snugly against the head rest of his seat. Turning on his laptop, he opened the files he'd uploaded a couple of hours earlier from his camera.

He was more than pleased with the photographs. They were clear and sharp, with the date and time they were taken on the top corner of each image. There could be absolutely no doubt about their authenticity. Looking at the last picture that showed Georgio Stephano, hands outstretched, Stone's attention was drawn once more to the ring. He would delete that picture – he would not show it to his client. The ring was an unexpected bonus and he wasn't prepared to share it.

He switched the camera into video mode for a few seconds to show the recording of blood flowing from Georgio's crumpled body, another verification of the job he'd completed.

Shutting his laptop, he reached into his pocket. He had wrapped the ring in a soft, protective cloth before leaving the house. He had not had time to examine it closely until now and, in the empty section of the carriage where he was sitting, he could look at it without prying eyes.

During his life Stone had travelled all over the world, yet he had never seen such an extraordinary ring, not even in the finest galleries and museums. He could hardly believe his luck that such an insignificant man had been wearing a small fortune on his finger.

Dazzling in its beauty, the workmanship was incredible. The likeness to the human eye was uncannily realistic; even though it was made with hard precious stones, it replicated a delicate organ of vision perfectly.

Staring at the sapphire iris, Stone felt a strange feeling of unease creep upon him. As he continued to look at the ring, it felt as if it had some innate ability to look directly back at him. Quite ridiculous, he told himself, yet even so he felt strangely uncomfortable.

Quickly wrapping up the ring, he placed it back in his pocket. He wasn't used to thoughts or feelings like this. He must be overtired, plus he had paid too much attention to churches, priests and old religious relics. These recent avenues of research had probably created fanciful notions in his subconscious.

Time for some refreshments, he thought. Steadying himself against the rocking motion of the high-speed train, he made his way towards the buffet car.

Chapter Eleven

In the next carriage were the two teenage girls who had burst into the first-class coach earlier. Sprawled lazily in their seats, they chatted animatedly, drinking coffee and munching peanuts. An elderly woman looked up at Stone and smiled at him, a glass of red wine in her hand. Ignoring her, he stared straight ahead, anxious to avoid any further eye contact. How much further, he thought, as he strode on.

He could have taken the complimentary first-class refreshments, but he needed to stretch his legs. He also found there was more choice in the buffet bar and, as he wasn't short of money, he could spend it as he wished.

Stone observed two men in their early twenties sitting opposite each other, laughing and joking. Further down the carriage, a mother was feeding her toddler. Most of the other passengers were quietly absorbed in their own thoughts, some sleeping, some reading, some doing crosswords. The carriage wasn't full and it was fairly quiet. The night train was often like this, and it was a good thing that there weren't many passengers. Although he felt his cover was virtually foolproof, if he wasn't remembered on this journey then so much the better.

On returning to his seat with a double whisky and a hot bacon roll, Stone looked out of the window. The train seemed to be going even faster, if that were possible. It was rushing along at an alarming speed. Lights from far away buildings flashed past in seconds and the carriage shook violently as it hurtled through the darkness.

He looked at the passengers further up his carriage. They seemed completely oblivious to the now almost deafening effects of the velocity of the train. Surely this wasn't normal? The carriage lights began to flicker and an empty water bottle rolled mechanically backwards and forwards on the floor. Even the heavily weighted window curtains were fluttering and swaying.

Despite the thunderously noisy train, the young woman with the cropped hair was still working away on her laptop, totally engrossed. The studious couple that had been reading earlier had dozed off, their books sliding perilously close to the edge of the table in front of them. The man in the charcoal suit was chatting on his mobile, his voice inaudible against the noise of the train. None of them seemed to be taking any notice of the train's rocket-like force.

Relax, Stone told himself. Trains go at an incredibly high speed nowadays and anyway, nobody else seemed bothered. He took a swig of the whisky and unwrapped his food. Sometimes the simplest food tastes best, he thought, as he bit into the hot, greasy sandwich. Although he liked expensive clothes, the latest computers and phones and the best restaurants, he wasn't comfortable in the pigeonhole of the middle classes. 'I'm not in any kind of box,' he often used to proclaim to his now-estranged family. He didn't get along with any of them: his mother, who'd always worried about him; his father when he was alive, or his younger sister. They complained that he was cold, uncaring and ungrateful. As a child, he had never been affectionate, and he was frequently accused of being cruel and heartless as he grew up.

When his father had died, Stone had just shrugged his shoulders, never showing any emotion or empathy. How could he? He didn't feel a thing. He hadn't experienced 'grief' as described by others. Life was all about getting what you wanted. No room for nostalgia or other such niceties. If that meant trampling over someone else to get a result, that was the logical thing to do. Why waste time pretending to care about others?

It was the same with women. He felt attraction, yes; love, no. If a woman had a brain as well as looks, that kept Stone interested for a while, but it was always the same scenario: they would want commitment, love, marriage and all that rubbish. That was not for him. Women were just another commodity in Stone's eyes, to be used at his convenience.

After consuming his whisky, and feeling replete from the food, Stone began to feel tired once again despite the raging noise. Closing his eyes, he drifted off to sleep. The noise of the train faded away as his mind and body relaxed. Gone were the sounds of the woman tapping on her laptop. He vaguely heard a mobile phone ring faintly in the distance, but that disappeared as he succumbed to the comforting realms of deep sleep.

Chapter Twelve

Stone woke suddenly with a jolt. Instantly alert, he immediately sensed that something was very wrong. Looking at his watch, he saw that he'd only been asleep for about thirty minutes or so. The train was still hurtling along at speed yet, despite the noise, whistling and vibration, Stone sensed an eerie kind of silence in the carriage itself. He couldn't hear the young couple chatting to each other – perhaps they still were asleep? The man in the charcoal-grey suit had stopped talking on his mobile. There were no human sounds at all.

A sudden coldness ran through him. For some reason, he hardly dared to look up. Something seemed to be telling him that all was not as it should be. Stone was not a man of a nervous disposition, and nothing in life had ever fazed him, but his professional instinct now alerted him.

Looking apprehensively out of the window, he saw nothing but the darkest night he could ever have imagined. It was all encompassing; there was not even the faintest glimmer of light. If the train was passing through a tunnel then it was one of an incredible length because it seemed to be going on forever.

Stone reluctantly stood up and looked across to where the couple had been sitting. Their books lay on the table, still sliding about as the train hurtled along angrily, but the pair were nowhere in sight. Glancing at where the businessman had been sitting, he saw the remains of a half-empty beer bottle together with a pile of notes and the grey jacket, still neatly folded on the adjoining seat as it had been before. Where was he now?

The ringing of a mobile phone interrupted the eerie atmosphere. Stone recognised the ring tone as belonging to the woman who had been working at her computer – but she was also nowhere to be seen. Her mobile continued to ring but the call remained unanswered.

Feeling perplexed, Stone stepped out into the aisle and walked over to the woman's seat. Her phone lay abandoned on the table, together with her open laptop. Where was she? No one left valuables like those lying around, even if they had to make a sudden dash to the toilets.

Leaning over the computer, Stone felt a sudden wave of a fear rise in the back of his throat as he looked at the screen. For some reason the screensaver hadn't kicked in, and his eyes widened in astonishment as he instantly recognised the image displayed in full colour before him. He gasped in disbelief. It was a picture of exactly the same ring he had in his pocket!

Stone couldn't take his eyes off the glittering eye, staring back at him with such piercing intensity from the computer screen. Taking a sharp intake of breath, he saw there was also an article attached to the image with the disturbing heading in bold: **THE ALL-SEEING EYE.**

As he started to read the text, a cold chill enveloped his body. He tried in vain to digest the information written about the arresting treasure he had so recently removed from the lifeless finger of Georgio Stephano.

THE ALL-SEEING EYE

It is the symbol of a Supreme Being from great nations of antiquity. The open eye was chosen as the symbol of watchfulness, the eye of God, the symbol of Divine watchfulness and care of the universe. The use of the symbol in this sense is repeatedly to be found in the words of Hebrew writers. Thus, the writer of Psalm xxxiv, 15 says: 'The eyes of the Lord are upon the righteous, and his ears are open unto their cry.'

In medieval and Renaissance European iconography, the Eye was an image of the Christian Trinity. Seventeenth-century depictions of the Eye of Providence sometimes show it surrounded by clouds or sunbursts. The All-Seeing Eye is one of many forms of a reflective eye-charm used as a talisman against danger. In its protective role, the All-Seeing Eye appears on at least one North American 'Good-Luck Coin' to guard the bearer from evil or to avenge him.

Stone felt the hairs on the back of his neck stand up. The article went on to say that *'anyone causing harm to the bearer of the All-Seeing Eye, will reap consequences of the most unimaginable horror'.*

Chapter Thirteen

Stone shuddered, experiencing the nauseating fear that can only arise when inexplicable events of enormous magnitude occur. He looked around apprehensively. The whole situation was becoming weirder by the second.

In these peculiar circumstances, the last thing he wanted was for the woman to suddenly return and find him using her computer! But she was still nowhere to be seen and, for some unknown reason, he knew she wouldn't be back. He left the computer as he had found it, open and still displaying the image of the ring in frightening full colour.

Beads of cold perspiration collected on Stone's forehead as he wrestled with the situation in which he found himself. He was a man of relatively few emotions, yet what he had just read had impacted on him profoundly. His pulse raced as he tried desperately to make sense of all it. His mind darted from one outlandish possibility to another – but nothing was plausible! And where was everyone? Where had they gone? Had they been herded into another carriage further down the train? But why had they left their personal belongings and valuables behind? It would have taken only moments to gather them up.

There had to be a rational explanation. There had to be an answer – things like this didn't happen in Stone's ordered and organised world. Maybe he had slipped up this time and left behind some incriminating clues? But he couldn't believe he had done that – he had been so careful with his planning. Yet he had already made one glaring error today by not checking for potential traffic problems. That had never happened before and, because of that oversight, he had nearly missed his train!

Was he becoming complacent? Could the passengers have been warned somehow that a contract killer was on board? Had the ring been reported as stolen, and had the article been placed intentionally on the computer to let Stone know they were on to him? Perhaps that would explain why the passengers had suddenly vacated the carriage: they had been ordered to do so by the police.

So many questions were racing through his mind, none of which he could answer or make sense of. Logically, Stone knew that the timescale would have made any of those scenarios impossible. There was absolutely no way that he could be connected to the crime he'd committed only a few hours earlier.

He said to himself out loud, 'How could the police possibly discover the identities of my fellow passengers, let alone source the history of the ring and post it onto the web? There hasn't been time.'

The police would be at the church right now and their investigation only just starting. There was nothing, except the ring he'd stolen to connect him to the murder. But how and why should an article about it suddenly appear on a complete stranger's laptop, published and ready to read? Had the woman somehow seen him examining the ring and decided to research it? No, there was not the slightest possibility of that; Stone was completely obscured from view in his seat. He'd even checked the possibility of CCTV and knew he was safe where he was sitting.

Yet it was too much of a coincidence that the ring he had removed from Stephano's finger a couple of hours ago, a ring of such value and uniqueness, now stared back at him from the woman's laptop. Stone didn't believe in coincidences like this. And he didn't know how to fathom out the other mystery, the disappearance of his fellow passengers.

Someone was trying to stitch him up, that was for sure. When I get the bastard that's doing this, he will wish he'd never been born, Stone thought.

Stone would have noticed immediately if anyone had walked past him while he looked at the photographs of the murder on his computer. His computer had been securely shut and put into its case when he'd taken a nap. The ring had been hidden deep in his pocket; to all intents and purposes, he looked like an affluent businessman, impeccably dressed, keeping himself to himself.

Thoughts came flooding in as Stone tried to reconcile the meaning of all this. There was nothing for it: he would have to check the adjoining carriages, the ones that were half full when he'd walked through them to the buffet car earlier.

With great apprehension, Stone approached the interconnecting door to the next carriage. It opened automatically as the motion sensors detected his presence. As he entered, he heard the woman's mobile phone start ringing behind him.

The train suddenly gave a lurch, curving sharply as it sped thunderously along the twisting tracks. Clinging on to a handrail, Stone felt the colour drain from his face as he took in the scene before him. The seats where the two teenage girls had been sitting lay abandoned. A half-drunk cup of coffee was still steaming, and a packet of peanuts lay strewn across the table. There was no sign of the girls.

As Stone walked cautiously through the carriage, he saw that the passengers' belongings still remained. In the luggage racks above empty seats were an assortment of bags, cases and umbrellas. On another table were the remains of a half-eaten sandwich, a glass of red wine and a magazine. He remembered the elderly woman who had smiled at him when he'd passed through earlier, and the two men in their twenties who were laughing and joking. They had also vanished, along with the mother and her toddler!

As Stone quickly scanned the rest of the carriage it was the same throughout; there was evidence of recent occupation but not a single passenger. The carriage ahead of this one was also empty; he could see it through the interconnecting doors!

The train hurtled along even more violently than before. Wheels screeched in a loud whine, like an animal in pain. Yet above the crashing crescendo, the deafening noise, it was the sinister emptiness that spoke the loudest to Stone. He turned around and ran as fast as he could, back to his own carriage.

Chapter Fourteen

But if thou do that which is evil, be afraid; for he beareth not the sword in vain: for he is the minister of God, a avenger to execute wrath upon him that doeth evil. (Romans 13:4)

Panic and confusion took hold of Stone. There was no way he could investigate these unnerving events any further. He had to sit and think, try reasoning them out, look for an explanation.

There *had* to be an answer to all of this he told himself. There *must* be. Yet how could anyone achieve this? Racking his brains, he collapsed into his seat, trying to process the bizarre events that were occurring. Was this some kind of sophisticated revenge for something he'd done in the past? But why now? And anyway, there was nothing to link him to any past crimes.

For his own peace of mind, for his own sanity, he had to get to the bottom of what had happened in the train very quickly. He checked his phone for messages but there were none. He scrolled through the internet for breaking news but, as he expected, there were no reports of his crime as yet. There were no stories about passengers in danger on a train having to leave in an emergency. What was happening? It was totally inexplicable, yet he had to get a grip; he must calm himself.

The lights in the carriage suddenly dimmed and the sound of screeching brakes assaulted Stone's ears as the train slowed down. After a few minutes, it braked to a crawl.

Curiously, he looked out of the window and saw another train was drawing parallel on the adjacent track. He stared into the brightly lit carriages packed with passengers. Slowing almost to a stop, he saw an elderly woman drinking a glass of red wine and eating a sandwich. Next was a young mother he vaguely remembered, feeding a toddler. She looked up at him as the train inched along, but gave no sign of recognition. A couple of teenage girls, sprawled out in their seats and eating a bag of peanuts, also looked familiar but soon slid out of view.

Stone's heart was pounding. The train continued to inch along and, as the next compartment drew alongside, he froze with horror and disbelief.

The woman with the boyish cropped hair, who'd been tapping away at her computer less than half an hour ago was in the other train! She looked up momentarily and stared blankly at him through the window, then resumed working on her laptop. But her laptop was here! He could still see it. He must be going mad! As the train continued to inch its way along, Stone recognised the businessman in his forties scribbling notes as before and still drinking a beer, his jacket folded neatly beside him.

Stifling the scream that rose to the back of his throat, Stone saw the young studious couple reading their textbooks. They looked up at him briefly, giving him a cold stare before disappearing into the night as the train rumbled past. Stone felt his nausea increase – he needed to get up and go to the washroom before he vomited. But before he could move, the lights suddenly turned off. The carriage was now in complete darkness.

Did such a thing as payback, as karma, occur in the modern world? Was there an inevitable consequence for what Stone had done in the past? He had never had anything to do with religion, the supernatural or anything of that nature, yet for the first time he began to question the possibility of their existence.

The train started to pick up speed once again but the lights remained off. A phone started to ring – it was the phone belonging to the young woman who owned the laptop. Shakily, Stone stood up. He could see a faint glow on the table from the laptop screen and the phone that lay beside it. Slowly he walked towards them, his whole body trembling. Picking the phone up, he hesitantly answered it. 'Yes?' he asked nervously.

There came a noise not unlike that of an old, creaking, wooden boat being tossed about in stormy seas. Stone listened to a moaning wail of wind and crashing waves. 'Who is this?' he asked.

Then a voice – a rasping, croaking, inhuman sound – replied. It penetrated his eardrums like tortured metal. 'Your time has come to an end, Mr Stone.' The words were spoken slowly, deliberately. 'Your malevolent deeds will not go unpunished. Be assured, there is no escape for you.'

The phone went dead. Stone quickly checked where it had come from but the screen said 'Caller Unknown'.

Walking unsteadily back to his seat, he could barely see because the carriage was so dark. All of a sudden there was a noise, the hiss of the interconnecting door opening at the other end of the carriage. Someone was approaching. Stone's jarred nerves tensed even further as he tried to fight off an overwhelming wave of terror.

A pungent stench of decay filled his nostrils and then a mysterious grey light appeared, spreading dense swirls of curling mist throughout the carriage. Seconds later, he heard the most sickening words, words that immersed him in complete and abject fear of what was to come. *'Tickets please.'*

It came from that hideous rasping voice, the same voice he had heard on the woman's phone a short while ago. Stone knew that a terrifying fate was close at hand. There was no escape, nothing he could do. He braced himself for the unknown force, the horrifying entity that was heading towards him from the far end of the dark empty carriage.

Chapter Fifteen

Some weeks later, Abbot Alwin went to retrieve some papers from his walnut desk. Opening a drawer, he immediately noticed the small jewellery box inside had moved slightly from its usual position. Looking inside, he saw the ring glinting there before him. 'You've completed your mission then,' the abbot said. He knew that what had happened to Georgio was because of the All-Seeing Eye, and yet he'd had no idea it would end this way.

Unfortunately, poor Georgio had been the sacrificial lamb.

'I thought he might have been saved,' said Abbot Alwin softly, looking at the ring. 'But there must have been reasons beyond my understanding. And, of course, further atrocities by that monster of a man Patrick Stone have been prevented. It is not for me to question the reasons why.'

The police had informed the monastery of the demise of their former brother and the small community of monks were deeply shocked and saddened. The authorities were continuing to investigate his murder and also a bizarre case of unexplained death to another man on the same day.

The only remains of Patrick Stone were his belongings and his charred skeleton – yet his clothes were intact. How he had died was a mystery. He was found in a sitting position, in a first-class railway carriage, with no scorched or burnt seats around him…

About the Author

Carolyn Stubbs is a freelance writer, a professional artist, and worked as an advertising copywriter for several years. Her other published work includes 'The Beach' a surreal short story, 'Living Tavistock' which she also illustrated and many features in magazines and journals.

The inspiration for 'Death Strikes Back' came from writing the storyline for the short supernatural film 'Underground' which won several awards at the European Short Film Festival.

As an artist Carolyn received the Wessex Watermark National Award for her environmental artwork 'Yesterday, Today, the Future…' and wrote an accompanying story to explain the futuristic images on the triptych. Her paintings and paper sculptures have been exhibited through-out the UK and abroad.

Carolyn has a love of nature and wildlife that can be seen in many of her artworks.

Author Website: http://www.carolynstubbs.co.uk